RUMPTY-DUDGET'S TOWER

RUMPTY-DUDGET'S TOWER

BASED ON THE FAIRY TALE BY
JULIAN HAWTHORNE

RETOLD AND ILLUSTRATED BY
DIANE GOODE

ALFRED A. KNOPF · NEW YORK

THIS IS A BORZOI BOOK
PUBLISHED BY ALFRED A. KNOPF, INC.

Text copyright © 1987 by Alfred A. Knopf, Inc.
Illustrations copyright © 1987 by Diane Goode
All rights reserved under International and Pan-American
Copyright Conventions. Published in the United States by
Alfred A. Knopf, Inc., New York, and simultaneously in
Canada by Random House of Canada Limited, Toronto.
Distributed by Random House, Inc., New York.
Manufactured in Singapore
Book design by Mina Greenstein

1   3   5   7   9   10   8   6   4   2

Library of Congress Cataloging-in-Publication Data
Goode, Diane. Rumpty-Dudget's tower.
Summary: When young Prince Henry is carried off to the
tower of the wicked dwarf Rumpty-Dudget, his brother
and sister must complete several difficult tasks to bring
about his freedom. [1. Fairy tales]
I. Hawthorne, Julian, 1846–1934. Rumpty-Dudget's tower.
II. Title. PZ8.G63Ru 1987 [Fic] 85-8575
ISBN 0-394-87862-0   ISBN 0-394-97862-5 (lib. bdg.)

For Peter Goode

I

LONG AGO, before you were born, a queen had three children, whose names were Prince Frank, Princess Hilda, and Prince Henry. Prince Frank was the eldest, Prince Henry was the youngest, and Princess Hilda was in between. They were the best children in the world, and the prettiest, and the cleverest; and they lived in the most beautiful palace ever built.

The palace garden was full of flowers and birds and fountains. In its center was a broad green lawn, and on the farther edge of this lawn was a high hedge, with only one round opening in the middle of it. But through this opening no one was allowed to pass; for the land on the other side belonged to a dwarf, whose name was Rumpty-Dudget, and whose only pleasure was in doing mischief. He was an ugly little dwarf, about as high as your knee, and all gray from head to foot. He lived in a gray tower, whose battlements could be seen from the palace windows. In this tower was a room with a thousand and one corners in it. In each of these corners stood a little child, with its face to the wall, and its hands behind its back. They were children that Rumpty-Dudget had caught trespassing on his grounds, and had carried off with him to his tower. In this way he had filled up one corner after another, until only one corner was left unfilled; and if he could catch a child to put in that corner, then Rumpty-Dudget would become master of the whole realm, and the beautiful palace would disappear, and the lovely garden would be changed into a desert, covered with gray stones and brambles. You may be sure, therefore, that Rumpty-Dudget tried very hard to get hold of a child to put in the thousand and first corner; but all the mothers were so careful, and all the children so obedient, that for a long time the thousand and first corner had remained empty.

II

WHEN Prince Frank and Princess Hilda and Prince Henry were still very young indeed, the queen, their mother, was obliged to make a long journey to a distant country, and to leave the children behind. They were not entirely alone, however; for there was a large cat with yellow eyes and a thick tail, to see that no harm came to them. His name was Tom.

One day, the unluckiest day in the whole year, Prince Frank, Princess Hilda, and Prince Henry were playing together on the broad lawn in the center of the garden. It was Rumpty-Dudget's birthday, and the only day in which he had power to creep through the round hole in the hedge and prowl about the queen's grounds. As ill fortune would have it, moreover, Tom was forced to be away on this day from sunrise to sunset, so that during all that time the three children had no one to take care of them. But they did not know there was any danger, for they had never yet heard of Rumpty-Dudget; and they went on playing together very affectionately, for up to this time they had never quarreled. The only thing that troubled them was that Tom the cat was not there to play with them; they all longed to see his yellow eyes and his thick tail, and to stroke his smooth back, and to hear his comfortable purr. However, it was now very near sunset, so they knew he would soon be back.

All at once Princess Hilda looked up and saw a strange dwarf standing close beside her. He wore a gray hat and beard, and on his back was a little gray hump. Princess Hilda was not frightened, for nobody had ever done her any harm; and besides, this strange little gray man, though he was very ugly, smiled at her from ear to ear, and seemed to be very good-natured. So she called to Prince Frank and Prince Henry, and they looked up too, and were no more frightened than Princess Hilda; and as the dwarf kept smiling from ear to ear, the three children smiled back at him. Meanwhile, the sun was slowly going down, and now its lower edge was just resting on the edge of the world.

You have heard of Rumpty-Dudget before, and therefore you know that this strange little gray dwarf was none other than he, and that although he smiled so pleasantly from ear to ear, he was really wishing to do the children harm, and even to carry one of them off to his tower to stand in the thousand and first corner. But he had no power to do this, so long as the children stayed on their side of the hedge; he must first tempt them to creep through the round opening, and then he could carry them wherever he pleased. So he held out his hand and said:

"Come with me, children. I have been wanting to meet you for such a long time; and if you will creep through that round opening in the hedge, I will show you something you never saw before."

The three children thought it would be very pleasant to see something they had never seen before, so they stood up and followed Rumpty-Dudget across the lawn. But they could not go very fast, for Prince Henry was hardly old enough to walk; meanwhile, the sun kept going down, and now its lower half was out of sight beneath the edge of the world. At last, however, they came to the round opening, and Rumpty-Dudget took hold of Prince Henry to lift him through it.

But just at that moment the last bit of the sun disappeared beneath the edge of the world, and instantly there was a great sound of meowing and spitting. Tom the cat came springing across the lawn, his great yellow

eyes flashing, his back bristling, and every hair upon his tail standing straight out. He flew at Rumpty-Dudget, and jumped upon his hump, and bit and scratched him soundly. At that Rumpty-Dudget screamed with pain, and dropped little Prince Henry, and vanished through the opening in the hedge.

But from the other side he threw a handful of black mud at the three children. A drop of it fell on Prince Frank's forehead, and another upon

Princess Hilda's nose, and a third upon little Prince Henry's chin; and each drop made a burning little black spot. And immediately Prince Frank, who had till then been the best little boy in the world, began to wish to order everybody about, and make them do what he pleased, whether they liked it or not; and Princess Hilda began to want all the good and pretty things that belonged to other people, in addition to what already belonged to her; and Prince Henry began to wish to do what he

was told not to do, and not to do what he was told to do. Such was the effect of the three black drops of mud.

III

ALTHOUGH Princess Hilda and her two little brothers were now no longer the best children in the world, they were still pretty good children and got along tolerably well together. But whenever the wind blew from the north, where Rumpty-Dudget's tower stood, Prince Frank ordered his brother and sister about, and tried to make them do what he pleased, whether they liked it or not; and Princess Hilda wanted some of the good and pretty things that belonged to her brothers; and Prince Henry would not do what he was told to do. And then, too, the spots on the children's faces became hotter and hotter, until at last they were ready to cry from pain and vexation. Those spots never disappeared altogether; and when the children asked Tom the cat if he could do anything to drive them away, he shook his furry head and said:

"I cannot, and as long as those spots are on your faces, a part of each of you belongs to Rumpty-Dudget. But when Frank becomes a horse, and Hilda a stick of firewood, and Henry a violin, then Rumpty-Dudget will lose his power over you, and the spots will vanish."

When the three children heard this, they were puzzled; for how could a little princess become a stick of firewood, or two little princes a horse and a violin? But that the cat would not tell them. He only touched each of

them on the heart and shook his head. No other answer would he give, so they were no wiser than before.

Thus time went steadily on until a year was past, and Rumpty-Dudget's birthday came round once more.

"I must leave you alone tomorrow," said Tom the day before, "from sunrise to sunset; but if you are careful to do as I tell you, all will be well. Do not go into the garden; do not touch the black ball that lies on the table in the nursery; and do not jump against the north wind."

Just as he finished saying these things, he sprang out of the room and disappeared.

All the next morning the children remembered what Tom had told them; they played quietly in the palace and did not touch the black ball on the nursery table. But when the afternoon came, Frank began to tire of staying shut up so long when out in the garden it was warm and pleasant and the wind blew from the south. And Hilda began to tire of her own playthings, and to wish that she might have the pretty black ball to toss up in the air and catch again. And Prince Henry began to tire of doing what he was told, and wished the wind would blow from the north, so that he might jump against it. At last they could bear it no longer, so Prince Frank stood up and said:

"Hilda and Henry, I order you to come out with me into the garden!"

And out they went; and as they passed through the nursery, Prince Henry knocked the black ball off the table, and Hilda picked it up. By the time they got to the garden, the three spots on their faces were blacker than ink and hotter than pepper; and, strange to say, the wind, which had been blowing from the south, now changed about and came from the north, where Rumpty-Dudget's tower stood. Nevertheless, the children ran about in the grass, tossing the black ball from one to another, and did not notice that every time it fell to the ground, it was a little nearer to the hedge which divided Rumpty-Dudget's land from the queen's garden. Then Prince Frank got the ball and kept tossing it up in the air and catching it again all by himself, without letting the others take their turns. They ran after him to get it away, and all three raced to and fro, without noticing that at every turn they were nearer and nearer to the high hedge, and to the round opening that led into Rumpty-Dudget's ground. After a long chase Princess Hilda and Prince Henry caught up with Prince Frank, and would have taken the black ball away from him; but he gave it a great toss upward, and it flew clear over the high hedge and came down upon the other side. Just then the sun dropped out of a cloud and rested on the edge of the world. It was three minutes to sunset.

IV

HE three children were very frightened when they saw where the ball had gone, and well they might be; for it was Rumpty-Dudget's ball, and Rumpty-Dudget himself was hiding on the other side of the hedge.

"It is your fault," said Princess Hilda to Prince Frank. "You threw it over."

"No, it is your fault," answered Prince Frank. "I shouldn't have thrown it over if you and Henry had not chased me."

"You will be punished when Tom the cat comes home," said Princess

Hilda, "and that will be in one minute, when the sun sets." For they had spent one minute being frightened, and another minute arguing.

Now all this time, Prince Henry had been standing in front of the opening in the hedge, looking through it to the other side, where he could see the black ball lying beside a bush. The north wind blew so strongly it took his breath away, and the spot on his chin burned him so that he was ready to cry with pain and vexation. By and by he could stand it no longer, and just as the last bit of sun sank out of sight beneath the edge of the world, he jumped through the round opening against the north wind, and ran to pick up the ball. At the same moment, Tom the cat came springing across the lawn, his yellow eyes flashing, his back bristling, and the hairs sticking straight out on his tail. But this time he came too late. For as soon as Prince Henry jumped through the hedge against the north wind and ran to pick up the black ball, out rushed Rumpty-Dudget from behind the bush, and caught him and carried him away to the thousand and first corner in the gray tower. As soon as the corner was filled, the north wind rose to a hurricane and blew away the beautiful palace and the lovely garden, and nothing was left but a desert covered with gray stones and brambles. The mischievous Rumpty-Dudget was now master of the whole realm.

Meanwhile, Prince Frank and Princess Hilda were sitting on a heap of rubble, crying as if their hearts would break, and the cat stood beside them wiping his great yellow eyes with his paw and looking very sorrowful.

"Crying will do no good," said the cat at last. "We must try to get poor little Henry back again."

"But how are we to do it?" said the children, crying even harder than before.

"Listen to me," replied the cat, "and do what I tell you, and all may yet be well. But first take hold of my tail, and follow me out of this desert to the borders of the great forest; there we can lay our plans without being disturbed."

With these words, Tom arose and held his tail straight out like the handle of a saucepan. The two children took hold of it, off they all went, and in less time than it takes to tell it they were on the borders of the great forest, at the foot of an immensely tall pine tree. The cat made Princess Hilda and Prince Frank sit down on the ground, and then sat down in front of them with his tail curled round his toes.

"The first thing to be done," said he, "is to get the Diamond Water-drop and the Golden Ivy seed. After that, the rest is easy."

"But where are the Diamond Waterdrop and the Golden Ivy seed?" asked the two children.

"One of you will have to go up to the kingdom of the Air-Spirits, above the clouds, to find out where the Diamond Waterdrop is," replied the cat. "And one of you will have to go down to the kingdom of the Gnomes, in the center of the earth, to find out where the Golden Ivy seed is."

"But how are we to get up to the Air-Spirits, or down to the Gnomes?" asked the children.

"I may be able to help you," answered the cat. "But while one of you is gone, the other must stay here and mind the magic fire which I shall kin-dle before we start; for if the fire goes out, Rumpty-Dudget will keep Henry forever. Run about and pick up all the dried sticks you can find, and pile them up in a heap, while I get the kindling ready."

In a very few minutes, a large heap of sticks had been gathered to-gether, as high as the top of Princess Hilda's head. Meanwhile, the cat had drawn a large circle on the ground with the tip of his tail, and in the cen-ter of the circle was the heap of wood. It had now become quite dark, but the cat's eyes burned as brightly as if two yellow lamps had been set in his head.

"Come inside the circle, children," said he, "while I light the kindling."

In they came, and the cat put the kindling on the ground and sat down in front of it with his nose resting against it, and stared at it with his flaming yellow eyes; and by and by it began to smoke and smolder, and at

last it caught fire and burned. "That will do nicely," said the cat. "Now put some sticks upon it." This was done, and the fire blazed away.

"And now there is no time to be lost," said Tom. "Hilda, stay beside this fire and keep it burning until I come back with Frank. Remember that if you let it go out, all will be lost; nevertheless, you must on no account go outside the circle to gather more wood if the sticks that are already here get used up. You may, perhaps, be tempted to do otherwise; but if you yield to the temptation, all will go wrong, and the only way your brother Henry can be saved will be for you to get into the fire yourself."

Princess Hilda did not much like the idea of being left alone in the woods all night; but since it was for her brother's sake, she consented, only she made up her mind not to use up the sticks of wood too quickly, or to go outside the ring. Frank and Tom the cat bade her farewell, and the cat stretched out his tail as straight as the handle of a saucepan. Frank took hold of it, and away! right up the tall pine tree they went and were out of sight in the twinkling of an eye.

V

AFTER climbing upward for a long time, they came at last to the tiptop of the pine tree, which was on a level with the clouds. The cat waited until a large cloud sailed along near them, and then, bidding Frank to hold on tight, they sprang together, and alighted very cleverly on the cloud's edge. Off it sailed and soon brought them to the kingdom of the Air-Spirits.

"Now, Frank," said the cat, "you must go the rest of the way alone. When you have found the queen of the Air-Spirits, ask her where the Diamond Waterdrop is. But be careful not to sit down, however much you may be tempted to do so; for if you do, your brother Henry never can be saved."

Prince Frank did not much like the idea of going on alone; but since it was for his brother's sake, he consented; only he made up his mind not to

sit down, no matter what happened. So he bade the cat farewell and walked off.

Before long he came to a large star, and there was the queen of the Air-Spirits sitting atop it. As soon as she saw Prince Frank, she said:

"You have come a long way, and you look very tired. Come here and sit down beside me."

"No, Your Majesty," replied Prince Frank, though he was really so tired he could hardly stand. "There is no time to be lost; where is the Diamond Waterdrop?"

"That is a foolish thing to come after," said the queen. "However, sit down here and let us talk about it. I have been expecting you."

But Prince Frank shook his head.

"Listen to me," said the queen. "I know that you like to order people about, and to make them do what you please. If you will sit down here, I will let you command the Air-Spirits instead of me, then everybody shall do what you please, whether they like it or not."

When Prince Frank heard this, for a moment he was very much tempted to do as the queen asked him. But the next moment he remembered his poor little brother Henry, standing in the thousand and first corner of Rumpty-Dudget's tower, with his face to the wall and his hands behind his back. This so saddened him that his eyes filled with tears, and he said:

"O Queen of the Air-Spirits! I am so sorry for my little brother that I do not care any longer to make people mind me; I only want the Diamond Waterdrop so that Henry may be saved from Rumpty-Dudget's tower. Can you tell me where it is?"

Then the queen smiled and said: "It is on your own cheek!"

Prince Frank was so astonished that he could only look at the queen without speaking.

"Yes," continued the queen, "you might have searched throughout all the kingdoms of the earth and air, and yet never have found that precious Drop, had you not loved your little brother so. That tear upon your cheek, which you shed for love of him, is the Diamond Waterdrop. Keep it in this little crystal bottle; be gentle and strong, and sooner or later Henry will be free again."

As she spoke she held out a little crystal bottle, and the tear from Prince Frank's cheek fell into it, and the queen hung it about his neck by a silver chain, and kissed him, and bade him farewell.

It was not long before he arrived at the cloud which had brought him to the kingdom of the Air-Spirits, and there he found Tom the cat awaiting him. Tom got up and stretched himself as Prince Frank approached, and when he saw the little crystal bottle hanging round his neck by its silver chain, he said:

"So far, all has gone well; but we have still to find the Golden Ivy seed. There is no time to be lost, so catch hold of my tail and let us be off."

With that he stretched out his tail and Prince Frank took hold of it. They sprang off the cloud and away! down they went till it seemed to him as if they never would be done falling. At last, however, they alighted softly on the top of a haymow, and in another moment were safe on the earth again.

Close beside the haymow was a fieldmouse's hole, and the cat began scratching at it with his two forepaws, throwing up the dirt in a heap be-

hind, till in a few minutes a great passage was made to the center of the earth.

"Keep hold of my tail," said the cat, and into the passage they went.

It was quite dark inside, and if it had not been for the cat's eyes, which shone like two yellow lamps, they might have missed their way. As it was, however, they got along famously, and pretty soon arrived at the center of the earth, where the kingdom of the Gnomes was.

"Now, Prince Frank," said the cat, "you must go the rest of the way alone. When you have found the Gnome king, ask him where the Golden Ivy seed is. But be careful to do everything that he bids you, no matter how little you may like it; for if you do not, your brother Henry can never be saved."

Prince Frank did not much like the idea of going on alone; but since it was for his brother's sake, he consented; only he made up his mind to do everything the king bade him, whatever happened. Before long he met a Gnome, who was running along on all fours.

"Can you show me where to find the Gnome king?" asked Prince Frank.

"What do you want with him?" asked the Gnome.

"I want to ask him where the Golden Ivy seed is," answered Prince Frank.

"He works in that great field over yonder," said the Gnome, "but unless you walk on all fours I don't believe he will tell you anything."

Prince Frank thought walking on all fours sounded exceedingly foolish, so he went onward just as he was.

At last he arrived at the field and walked in; and there was the king on all fours in the midst of it. As soon as he saw Prince Frank, he said:

"Get down on all fours this instant! How dare you come into my kingdom walking upright?"

"Oh, Your Majesty," said Frank, though he was frightened at the way the king spoke, "there is no time to be lost; where is the Golden Ivy seed?"

"The Golden Ivy seed is not given to proud or disobedient people," replied the king. "Get down on all fours at once, or else go about your business!"

Then Prince Frank remembered what the cat had told him, and he got down on all fours without a word.

"Now, listen to me," said the king. "I shall harness you to that plow in the place of my horse, and you must draw it up and down over this field

until the whole field is plowed, while I follow behind with the whip. Come! There is no time to be lost."

When Prince Frank heard this he felt tempted for a moment to refuse; but then he remembered his poor little brother Henry standing in the thousand and first corner of Rumpty-Dudget's tower, so he said:

"O King of the Gnomes! I am so sorry for my little brother that I will do as you bid me, and all I ask in return is that you will give me the Golden Ivy seed, so that Henry may be saved."

The king said nothing, but harnessed Frank to the plow just as if he were a horse. Then Prince Frank drew the plow up and down over the field until the whole field was plowed, while the king followed behind with the whip. At last the king freed Prince Frank from his trappings and told him to go about his business. "But where is the Golden Ivy seed?" cried Prince Frank.

"I have no Golden Ivy seed," answered the king. "Ask yourself where it is!"

Then poor Prince Frank's heart was broken, and he sank down on the ground sobbing, "Oh, what shall I do to save my little brother!" At that the king smiled upon him and said:

"Put your hand over your heart, Frank, and see what you find there."

Prince Frank was so surprised that he could say nothing; but he put his hand over his heart, and felt something fall into his palm, and when he looked at it, behold! it was the Golden Ivy seed.

"Yes," said the king, "you might have searched through all the kingdoms of the earth and air, and never have found that precious seed, had you not loved your brother so much that you let yourself be driven like a horse in the plow for his sake. Keep the Golden Ivy seed in this little box; be humble and patient, and sooner or later your brother will be free."

As he spoke he fastened a little golden box to Prince Frank's belt with a jeweled clasp, and kissed him, and bade him farewell.

It was not long before Prince Frank arrived at the mouth of the passage by which he had descended to the kingdom of the Gnomes, and there he found Tom the cat awaiting him. Tom got up and stretched himself as Prince Frank approached, and when he saw the golden box, he said:

"So far, all goes well; but now we must see whether or not Princess Hilda has kept the fire going; there is no time to be lost, so catch hold of my tail and let us be off."

With that, he stretched out his tail. Prince Frank took hold of it, and away they went back through the passage again, and were out at the other end in the twinkling of an eye.

VI

OW, after Princess Hilda had seen Prince Frank and the cat disappear up the trunk of the tall pine tree, she had sat down beside the fire, which blazed away furiously. Every once in a while she took a stick from the pile and put it in the flame; but she was very careful not to step outside the circle which the cat had drawn with the tip of his tail. So things went on for a very long time, and Princess Hilda began to get very sleepy, for never before had she sat up so late; but still Prince Frank and the cat did not return, and she knew that if she were to lie down to take a nap, the fire might go out before she woke up again, and then Rumpty-Dudget would have her brother Henry in his power forever. So Hilda kept putting fresh sticks in the flames, though it was all she could do to keep her eyes open; and the fire kept on burning.

But after another very long time had gone by, Princess Hilda found that there was only one stick left of all that she and Frank had gathered together. At this she was very much frightened, and knew not what to do; for when that stick was burned up, as it soon would be, what was she to do to keep the fire going?

In order to make the stick last as long as possible, she broke it into tiny pieces, and put only one piece in the flame at a time; but after a while, all but the last piece was gone, and when she had put that in, Princess Hilda sat down in despair and cried with all her might. Just then she heard a voice calling her, and, looking up, she saw a little gray man standing just outside the circle, with a great bundle of sticks in his arms. Princess Hilda's eyes were so full of tears that she did not see that the little gray man was Rumpty-Dudget.

"What are you crying for, my dear little girl?" asked the gray dwarf, smiling from ear to ear.

"Because I have used up all my wood," answered Princess Hilda, "and if the fire goes out, my brother Henry cannot be saved."

"That would be too bad, surely," said the dwarf. "Luckily, I have got an armful, and when these are gone I will get you some more."

"Oh, thank you—how kind you are!" cried Princess Hilda, jumping up in great joy and going to the edge of the circle. "Give them to me now, for there is no time to be lost; the fire is just going out."

"I can't bring them in," replied the dwarf. "I have carried them all the way from the other end of the forest, and that is far enough; surely you can come the rest of the way yourself."

"Oh, but I must not come outside the circle," said Princess Hilda, "for the cat told me that if I did, all would go wrong."

"What does a cat know about anything?" asked the dwarf. "Look at your fire. It will not burn one minute longer; and you know what will happen then."

Princess Hilda did not know what to do; but anything seemed better than to let the fire go out; so she put one foot outside the circle and stretched out her hand for the wood. Then the dwarf gave a loud laugh and threw the wood away as far as he could; and rushing into the circle, he began to stamp out the little of the fire that was left.

Then Princess Hilda remembered what the cat had told her; she turned and rushed back into the circle; and as the last bit of flame flickered in the fire she laid herself down upon it like a bit of firewood. Immediately Rumpty-Dudget gave a loud cry and disappeared; and the fire blazed up brightly with poor little Princess Hilda in the midst of it!

VII

UST THEN, and not a moment too soon, along came Tom the cat through the forest, with Prince Frank holding on to his tail. As soon as they were within the circle, Tom dug a little hole in the ground with his two forepaws, and said:

"Give me the Golden Ivy seed, but make haste; for Hilda is burning for Henry's sake!"

So Prince Frank gave him the Seed; and he planted it quickly in the little hole and covered the earth over it, and then said:

"Give me the Diamond Waterdrop, but make haste; for Hilda is burning for Henry's sake!"

So Prince Frank made haste to give him the Drop; and Tom poured half of it on the fire and the other half on the place where the Seed was planted. And immediately the fire was put out, and there lay Princess Hilda all alive and well; and the mark of Rumpty-Dudget's mud on her nose was burned away. Up she jumped and she and Prince Frank and Tom all kissed each other heartily; and then Princess Hilda said:

"Why, Frank! The black spot that you had on your forehead has gone away too."

"Yes," said the cat. "That happened when the king of the Gnomes kissed him. But now make yourselves ready, children; for we are going to take a ride to Rumpty-Dudget's tower!"

The two children were very much surprised when they heard this, and looked about to see what they were to ride on. But behold! The Golden Ivy seed, watered with the Diamond Waterdrop, was already growing and sprouting, and a strong stem with bright golden leaves had pushed itself

out of the earth, and was creeping along the ground in the direction of Rumpty-Dudget's tower. The cat put Prince Frank and Princess Hilda on the two largest leaves, and got on the stem himself, and so away they went merrily, and in a very short time the Ivy had carried them to the tower gates.

"Now jump down," said the cat.

Down they all jumped; but the Golden Ivy kept on, and climbed over the gate, and crept up the stairs and along the narrow passageway, until the ivy had reached the room with the thousand and one corners, in the midst of which Rumpty-Dudget was standing; and all around were the poor little children whom he had caught,
standing with their faces to the

wall and their hands behind their backs.

When Rumpty-Dudget saw the Golden Ivy creeping toward him, he was very frightened and tried to run away; but the Ivy caught him and twined around him, and squeezed him tighter and tighter, until all the mischief was squeezed out of him. And since Rumpty-Dudget was made of mischief, when all the mischief was squeezed out of him, there was no Rumpty-Dudget left! He was gone for-ever.

Instantly, all the children that he had kept in the thousand and one corners were free, and came racing and shouting out of the gray tower, with Prince Henry in front. When he saw his brother and sister, and they saw him, they all three hugged and kissed one another over and over again. At last Prince Frank said, "Why, Henry, the spot that was on your chin has gone away too!"

"Yes," said a voice, which Frank was certain he had heard somewhere before. "While he stood in the corner his chin rubbed against the wall, until the spot was gone; so now he no longer wishes to do what he is told not to do, or not to do what he is told to do. Now when he is spoken to, he answers sweetly and obediently, as a violin answers the bow when it touches the strings."

Then the children looked around, and there with a golden crown on her head and a loving smile in her eyes was their mother, the queen!

"Mama!" they cried, rushing into her outspread arms.

"My darlings!" she answered, kissing all three. "By Rumpty-Dudget's enchantments, I was unable to return to you for this long year, though my love has been with you always, and has followed you everywhere. But the power of your love for little Henry was so strong that it has broken Rumpty-Dudget's spell. Now at last you shall come home with me, for our palace and gardens have been restored, and all is now as it once was. Are you ready?"

"Oh, but where is Tom the cat?" cried all three children together. "We cannot be entirely happy without him." The queen laughed and kissed them, and said, "He is already there, waiting for us."

When the children heard this, they were perfectly contented. They clung about their mother's neck; she folded her arms around them, and soon they were back in the palace that had been their home. And there was Tom the cat to greet them, his great yellow eyes glowing and his thick tail waving in the air!

And there they all live happily, to this very day.

JULIAN HAWTHORNE

was born in Boston, Massachusetts, in 1846. His body of work includes stories, essays, and anthologies as well as two biographies of his father, the distinguished American author Nathaniel Hawthorne. *Rumpty-Dudget's Tower* first appeared in print in 1879, when it was serialized in *St. Nicholas* magazine, and was later published in book form.

Julian Hawthorne died in 1934.

DIANE GOODE

was born in New York City and studied painting and drawing at Les-Beaux-Arts in Aix-en-Provence, France. She has illustrated many highly praised books for children, including *When I Was Young in the Mountains,* winner of a 1983 Caldecott Honor Award and an American Book Award nomination, and *The Random House Book of Fairy Tales.*

Ms. Goode lives in New York State with her husband and young son.